About this Book

Everyone appreciates a little gratitude! Grandma for hosting a sleepover. Uncle Bob for mailing that $25 gift. Your friend, Sue, for taking the kids to preschool last week. In the age of e-mail, some say the hand written thank-you note is a rarity. That's why we've created Thank-U-Grams, a fun, quick way to continue the longstanding tradition of sending thanks. We've included both fill-in-the-blank cards and "regular" notes to appeal to all ages.

Thank-U-Grams

Marianne Richmond Studios, Inc.
420 N. 5th Street, Suite 840
Minneapolis, MN 55401
www.mariannerichmond.com

ISBN 0-9774651-1-X

Text and illustrations by Marianne Richmond

Book design by Meg Anderson

Printed in China

First Printing

Thanks for a great time!

Thanks for a great time!

Thank you very much

Thank You

Thank You

Thanks

Thanks for
the gift

Thank
You!

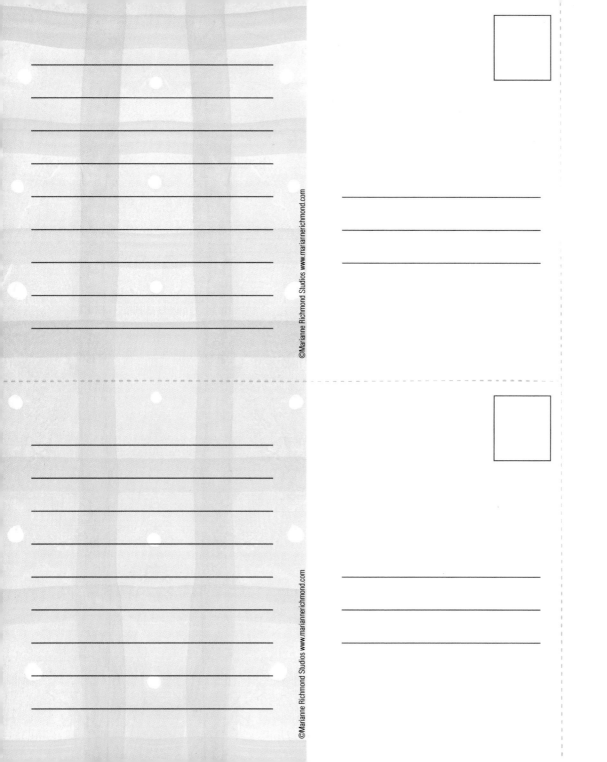

Thank You

THANK YOU

Thanks for a wonderful time

Thanks for a
wonderful time

Thanks for the gift

Thanks for
the gift

Thank you

very much!

THANK YOU VERY MUCH!

© Marianne Richmond Studios www.mariannerichmond.com

Dear_____,
Thank you for

_____

_____

Love,_____

Dear_____,
Thank you for

_____

_____

Love,_____

THANK YOU

Thanks for your friendship

Thanks for your hospitality

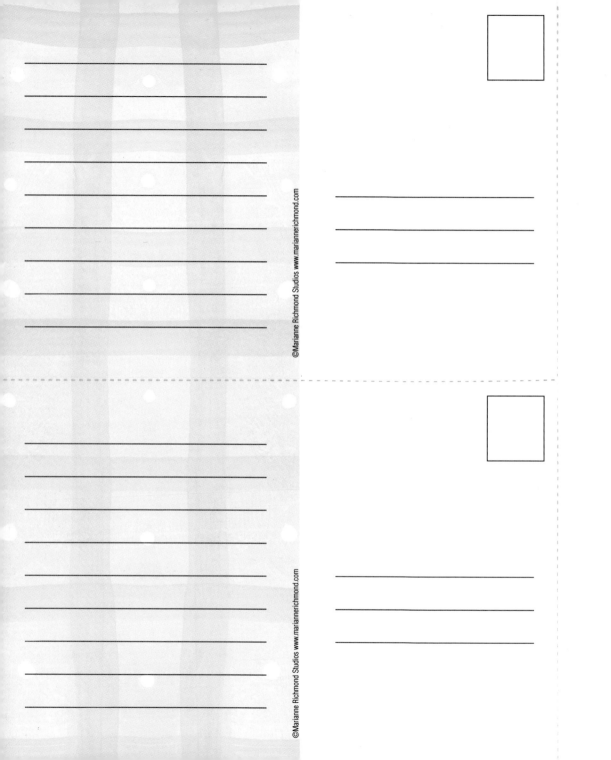

Thank You

Thank You

THANK
YOU

thank
you

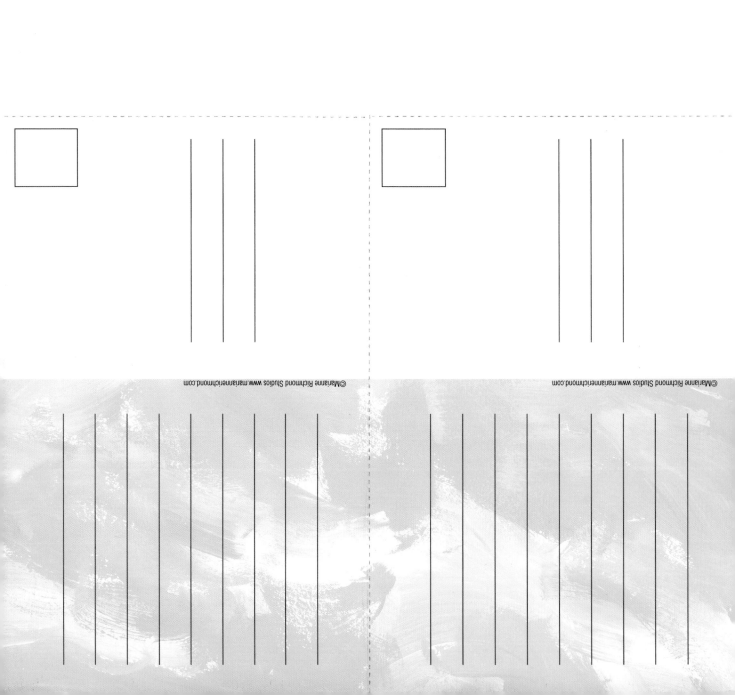

Dear_____,

Thank you for the

_____

from,

_____

Dear_____,

Thank you for the

_____

from,

_____

Thank You

Thank You